HOSIE'S AVIARY

ALSO ILLUSTRATED BY LEONARD BASKIN
Hosie's Alphabet

HOSIE'S AVIARY

Pictures by LEONARD BASKIN · Words mostly by

TOBIAS BASKIN & Lucretia, Hosie & Lisa Baskin

THE VIKING PRESS · NEW YORK

First Edition
Copyright © Leonard Baskin, 1979
All rights reserved · First published in 1979 by The Viking Press,
625 Madison Avenue, New York, N.Y. 10022 · Published simultaneously in Canada by
Penguin Books Canada Limited · Printed in U.S.A.
1   2   3   4   5   83   82   81   80   79

Library of Congress Cataloging in Publication Data
Baskin, Leonard. Hosie's aviary.
Summary: Text and pictures portray a variety of birds.
1. Birds—Juvenile literature. [1. Birds] I. Baskin, Tobias. II. Title.
QL676.2.B37   598.2   78-27027   ISBN 0-670-37965-4

List of Illustrations

Humminghumminghummhum minghum hum
ing birds humhum
hummingbirds inghum inghumming
humhumhum

The bald eaglet screaming for food:
the condition of growth—caught
and revealed

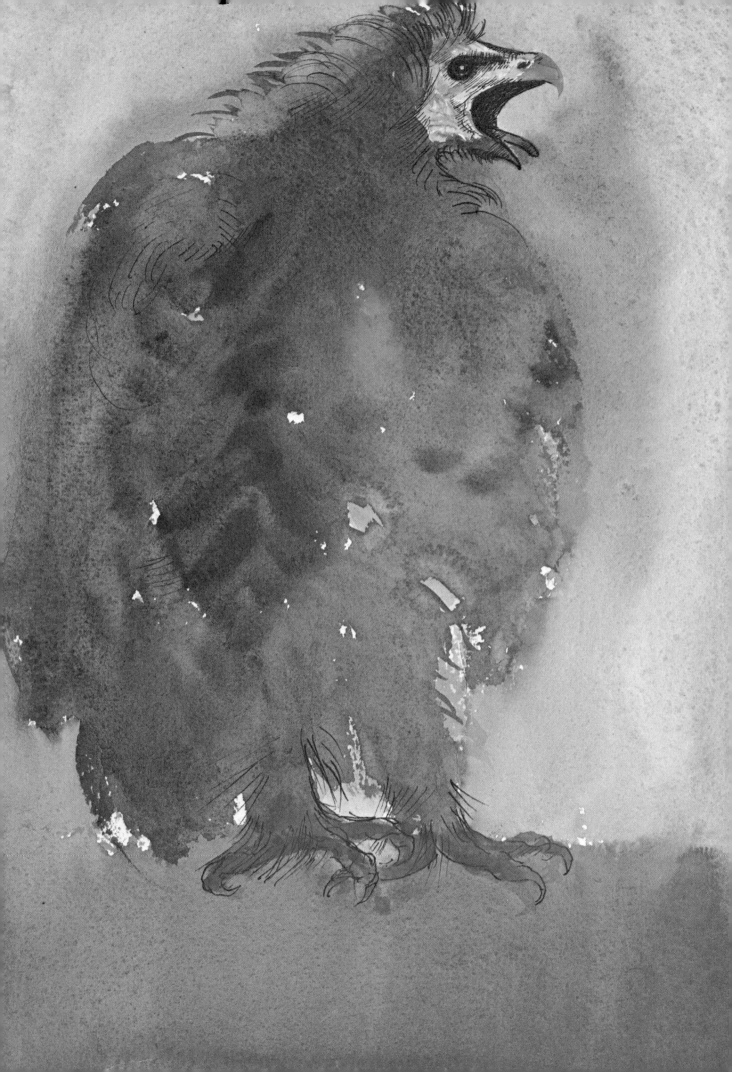

In layers of feathers
the oracle owl holds hidden
the secrets of might

KINGFISHER

If you don't finish your dinner
the kingfisher will
gobble
it
all
up

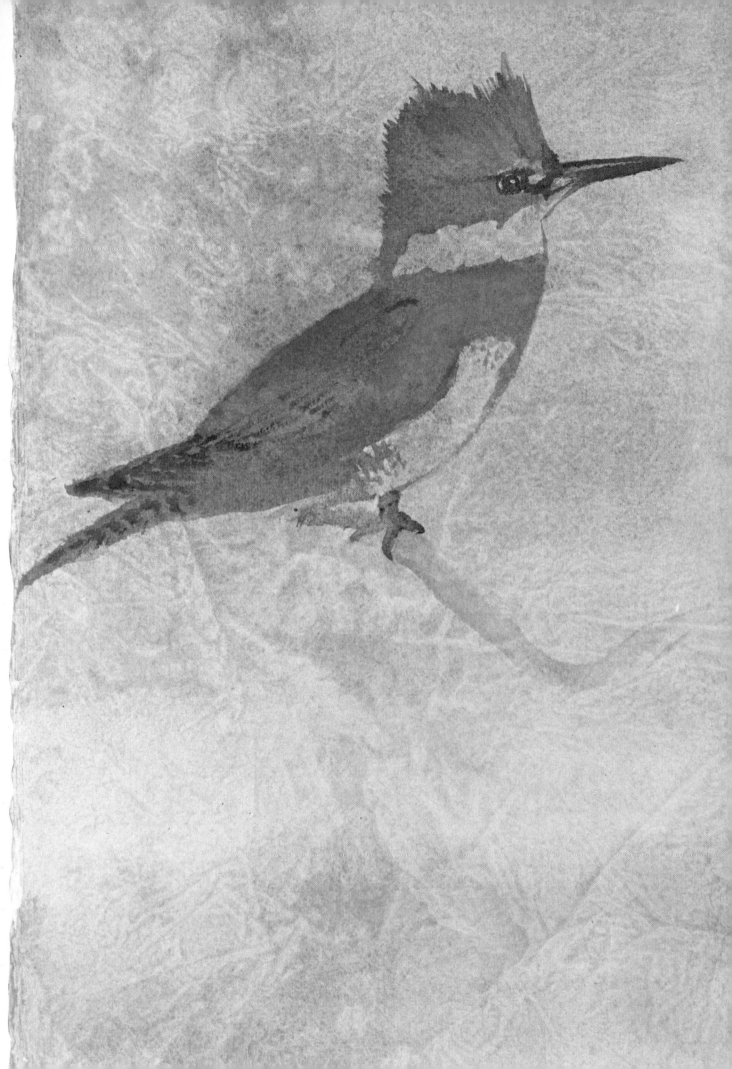

SHRIKE

The shrike
would kill you
and eat you
for Sunday dinner if
you were a little
shorter

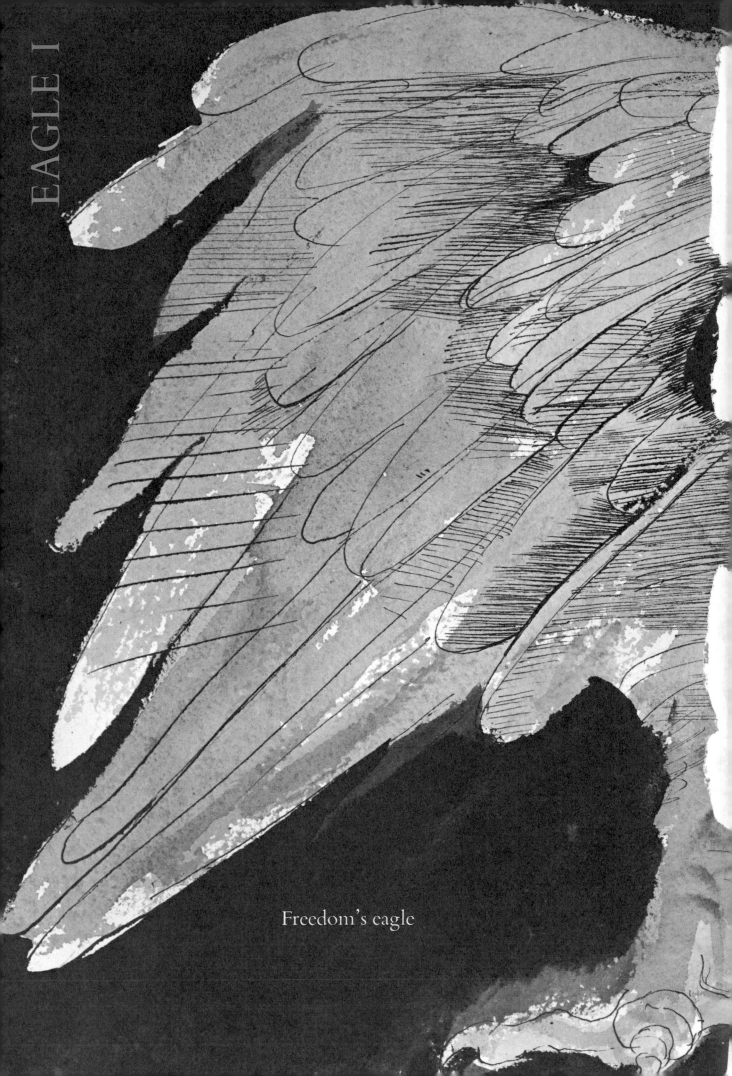

EAGLE I

Freedom's eagle

Long hair
and pencil bill,
does this egret write poems?

The eagle perches
on a branch of sun, up so high
that soon its patient blood
will start to boil

OWLphabet:

A waits

B sights

C soars

In the dark,
the yellow-crowned night heron
looms
on one leg
waiting for fish

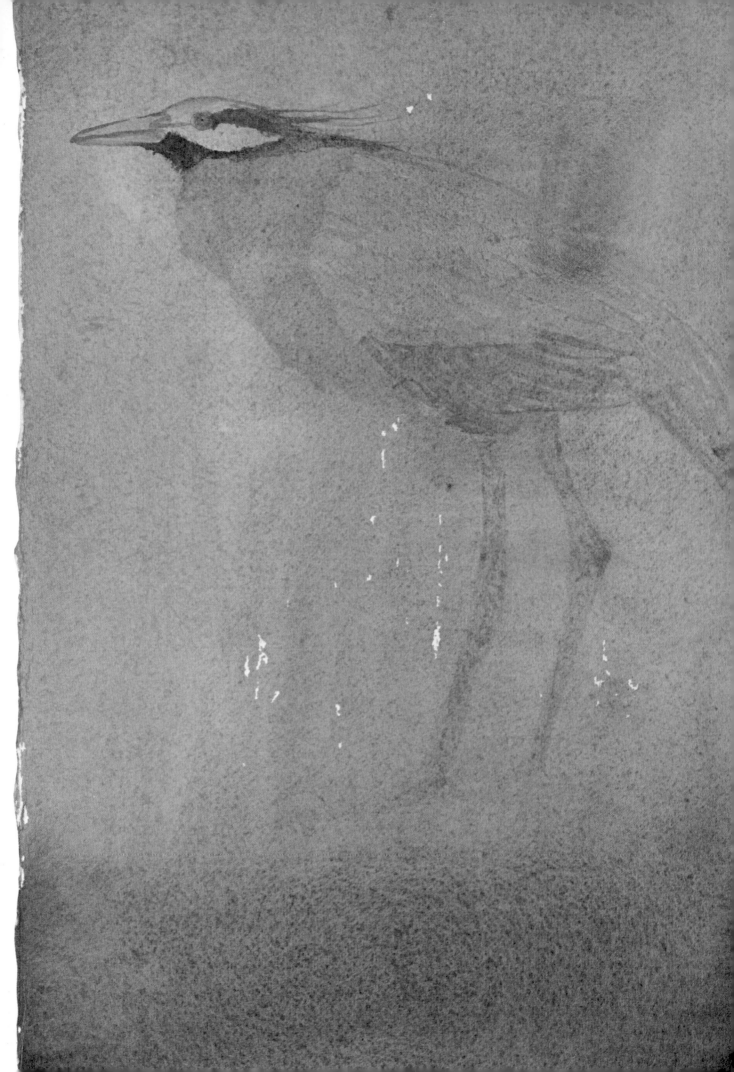

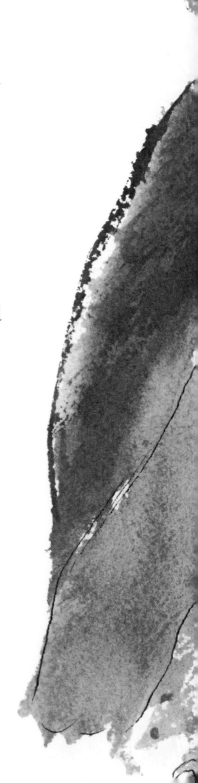

The barn owl
destroyer of vermin,
a deep-eyed hunter of old land

Aloo Alix Egiy
The beak of the secretary bird
vents raucous screams

The golden eaglet's upside down,
upside down,
upside down
The golden eaglet's upside down—
oops, all go flying!

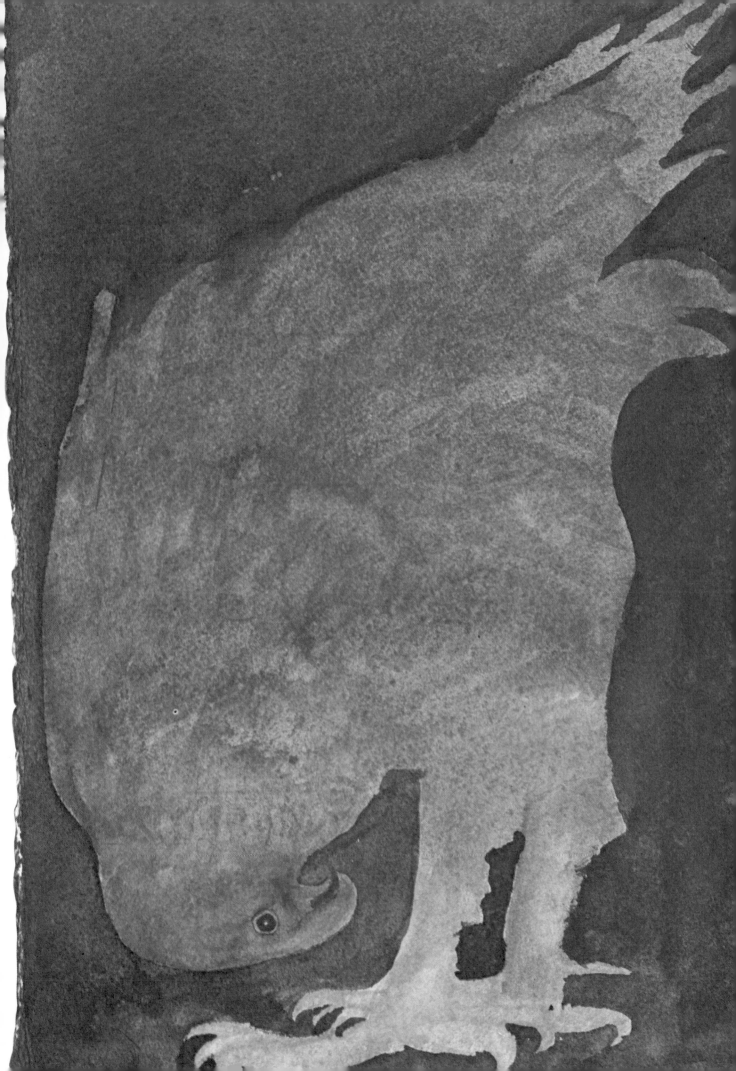

Finches—
they sing that all life is interdependent

The little blue heron
swallowed
the moon